Special thanks to Diane Reichenberger, Cindy Ledermann, Jocelyn Morgan, Kim Culmone, Tanya Mann, Emily Kelly, Sharon Woloszyk, Carla Alford, Rita Lichtwardt, Kathy Berry, Rob Hudnut, David Wiebe, Shelley Dvi-Vardhana, Gabrielle Miles, Rainmaker Entertainment, and Walter P. Martishius

Barbie
Mariposa
& the Fairy Princess

Adapted by Kristen L. Depken
Based on the screenplay by Elise Allen
Illustrated by Ulkutay Design Group

 A GOLDEN BOOK • NEW YORK

*I*n the kingdom of Flutterfield, there lived a beautiful Butterfly Fairy named Mariposa. One day, she and her friend Willa were on their way to the royal library, where Mariposa worked.

"Hi, Mariposa! Good morning!" called some passing Butterfly Fairies. Everyone in Flutterfield loved Mariposa.

Mariposa's pink puffball friend, Zee, told her that the queen wanted to see her.

"Did she say why?" asked Mariposa.

Zee shrugged, and the trio set out for the palace.

When Mariposa and her friends arrived at the palace, they were greeted by Queen Marabella and her son, Prince Carlos. Queen Marabella announced that she had selected Mariposa to be the royal ambassador to Shimmervale, the kingdom of the Crystal Fairies.

Most Butterfly Fairies had heard stories that Crystal Fairies were scary and cruel.

"All the horrible stories about Crystal Fairies are just that: stories," said Mariposa.

She explained that the Butterfly Fairies and the Crystal Fairies had once been allies. But then the king of the Crystal Fairies had accused the Butterfly Fairies of trying to steal the powerful Crystallites, which gave life to Shimmervale. After that, the Butterfly Fairies and the Crystal Fairies became sworn enemies.

"You will live with the royal family for one week and prove that Butterfly Fairies and Crystal Fairies can be friends," the queen told Mariposa.

Mariposa and Zee set off on their journey. To remind her of home, Mariposa brought a magical Flutter Flower from Flutterfield with her. After two days of traveling, they finally arrived in Shimmervale, where they met a nervous Crystal Fairy named Talayla.

"Don't hurt me!" cried Talayla when she spotted Mariposa and Zee.

"Of course we won't hurt you," replied Mariposa.

Relieved that the horrible rumors she had heard about Butterfly Fairies didn't seem to be true, Talayla took Mariposa and Zee on a tour of Shimmervale. "As you can see, every roof has a Crystallite, the main source of heat and power here in Shimmervale." Mariposa and Zee were amazed by the sparkling kingdom.

Not a single Crystal Fairy had come out to greet them, but as they flew past the castle, they saw a beautiful fairy waving from the window.

"I'm Catania," she told them before a voice from inside called her away. "Welcome to the kingdom!"

The last stop on Talayla's tour was the royal palace, where Mariposa would be staying. Talayla led Mariposa and Zee through magnificent hallways that shimmered with crystals of every color. When she got to Mariposa's room, she threw open the door excitedly. "Ta-da!"

Mariposa's jaw dropped, and Zee squealed in disgust. The room was decorated in dark, spooky colors. Spiky trees and thorny chairs made it look more like a haunted forest than a bedroom.

"I based it on everything we know about Butterfly Fairies," said Talayla.

"That was . . . thoughtful," said Mariposa. She was trying to be nice, but it was clear that Talayla didn't know much about Butterfly Fairies.

Later that day, Talayla took Mariposa to meet the king and princess of Shimmervale.

Mariposa and Zee excitedly followed Talayla to a majestic throne room. To Mariposa's surprise, the princess was the friendly fairy from the window! As the group prepared for a royal tea, Mariposa noticed that Catania couldn't fly on her own. Instead, she relied on a beautiful horse with wings.

"I love how the Crystallites shimmer in the sun," said Mariposa, reaching toward one.

"Do not touch that!" shouted King Regellius. "The Crystallites are only to be touched by Crystal Fairies!"

Mariposa shrank back, and her wings—which were much larger than Crystal Fairy wings—accidentally hit the king in the face.

"Oh no!" cried Mariposa. She spun around to apologize, but her wings bumped into everything—including the king. "Come, Catania!" the king said as he flew out of the room, leaving Mariposa and Zee behind. As Catania followed on her winged horse, she looked back at Mariposa apologetically.

Two days later, Mariposa had still not improved her standing with the king, so she was completely surprised to see her room redecorated.

"Did I get it right?" asked Princess Catania as she entered the room with her flying horse, Sylvie.

"Almost exactly!" exclaimed Mariposa. She didn't think she could love the room more, until Catania pulled aside a curtain to reveal a wall full of books. "This is incredible!"

"I like to read, too," Catania said with a smile. "I've been reading up on Flutterfield since I found out you were coming."

Catania was delighted to have met a fairy she had so much in common with. "I want to show you something," she told Mariposa. Sylvie gave her a concerned look. "Don't worry, Sylvie. We can trust Mariposa."

Catania led Mariposa to a garden high atop the palace, where a huge Crystallite glowed.

"This is the Heartstone, isn't it?" asked Mariposa.

"Yes," replied Catania. "It's the most powerful Crystallite we have."

Next, Catania took Mariposa to see the beautiful Glow Water Falls. The girls laughed and skipped Rainbow Rocks across the shimmering surface of the water.

"I've missed this place," Catania said with a sigh. "I haven't been here in years."

"Why has it been so long?" asked Mariposa.

Catania hesitated, then began to tell Mariposa about the last time she had visited the Falls.

"I was eight years old," said Catania. "My father and I were having a picnic when we saw something down below. It was an old woman. She asked for a Crystallite."

The woman was an evil fairy called Gwyllion. When King Regellius refused to give her a Crystallite, Gwyllion grew angry and cast a magic spell on the king, freezing him on the spot.

"I had to do something," said Catania. She flew at Gwyllion, but the old fairy froze her, too, and pulled her high above Glow Water Falls.

The king broke free of the spell, but he was too late. Gwyllion had thrown Catania to the ground.

Catania sounded terrified just talking about it. "I haven't flown since," she explained. "I'm too afraid." They didn't see Gwyllion again, but the king still worried that she would return.

"I want you to have this," Catania said. She gave Mariposa a beautiful Crystallite necklace.

"No Butterfly Fairy should ever take a Crystallite from Shimmervale," said Mariposa.

Catania insisted. "It's a friendship gift."

Mariposa thanked her, then took something from her pocket. "It's a Flutter Flower," she explained. "Maybe after I leave, it can remind you of me."

When the gifts were held close together, they began to glow.

Just then, Catania remembered that the palace's Crystal Fairy Ball was taking place that night! She and Mariposa hurried back to get ready and soon were dressed in gorgeous gowns that sparkled and shimmered.

Mariposa folded her wings down like a skirt so they wouldn't cause any more accidents.

"If you have to fold down your wings, I will, too," said Catania.

Unable to fly with her wings folded down, Mariposa climbed aboard Sylvie with Catania, and they flew into the ballroom. It was breathtaking! There were fairies dancing in midair and waiters fluttering around with trays full of fabulous food.

"I always loved dancing . . . ," Catania said wistfully as she watched the other fairies.

Mariposa had an idea.

"Let's dance!" she said. She flew to the floor and started dancing, and Catania soon joined in. The two fairies spun and twirled across the floor. It was the most fun either of them had had in a long time.

While they were dancing, the Crystallite necklace that Catania had given Mariposa fell to the floor.

"Mariposa, you stole a Crystallite after we welcomed you!" accused King Regellius.

"I gave it to her!" Catania said. "We were at Glow Water Falls, and—"

"Mariposa took you to Glow Water Falls? Unprotected?" the king boomed, furious at Mariposa.

"We weren't doing anything wrong," said Mariposa. "I understand why you're so protective—"

"You know nothing!" shouted the king. "You don't know what it's like to be responsible for a kingdom. Leave Shimmervale—and never come back!"

"Father!" protested Catania.

"Not now, Catania," said the king angrily.

"As you wish, Your Majesty," said Mariposa sadly. She flew out of the ballroom with Zee right behind her.

Mariposa gathered her belongings, and soon she and Zee were flying away from Shimmervale. They hadn't gotten far, however, when they spotted a strange creature and a large black bat flying in the opposite direction.

It was Gwyllion—and she was headed toward the palace!

"We have to warn the Crystal Fairies!" cried Mariposa.

Mariposa and Zee secretly began to follow Gwyllion. Suddenly, the wicked fairy stopped and waved a crooked staff in the air. A beam of green magic shot out and began turning all the Crystallites in its path to stone.

Mariposa and Zee gasped. Gwyllion was destroying Shimmervale!

Mariposa soon found Princess Catania and told her about Gwyllion. "Gwyllion's flying toward the Heartstone!" cried Catania. Just then, Gwyllion's huge bat crashed into Catania and Sylvie. They fell to the ground, and one of Sylvie's wings was hurt.

Mariposa took off toward the Heartstone. "Come fly with me!" she called to Catania. "You can do this."

But Catania was terrified. "I can't fly," she said, shaking her head.

There was no time to waste, so Mariposa flew toward Gwyllion, who was pointing her magic staff at the Heartstone.

"Stop!" cried Mariposa. But the evil fairy just cackled and blasted a beam of magic at Mariposa. The Butterfly Fairy fell to the ground, frozen.

Gwyllion turned back to the Heartstone, blasting it with magic. The glowing stone slowly started transforming into a hideous, cold rock.

Suddenly, Catania appeared above the Heartstone. She was flying—using her own wings! Catania dove toward Gwyllion and, in one swoop, broke her magic staff.

"Noooo!" cried Gwyllion as she fell off the terrace.

When the staff broke, so did Gwyllion's magic spell. Mariposa was able to move again. "You did it!" she exclaimed.

"Not fast enough," said Catania. She pointed to the Heartstone, which was now almost completely dark. "It's too late."

The Heartstone began to shake, and the kingdom turned cold and dark.

Just then, Mariposa noticed something glowing in Catania's pocket. "The Flutter Flower!" exclaimed Catania. She pulled it from her pocket and held it near the Heartstone. Something flickered inside the dark stone.

"Keep holding it close to the Heartstone!" said Mariposa.

The Heartstone continued to glow warmer and brighter, until a huge burst of beautiful rainbow light exploded from it, bringing all the other Crystallites back to life and illuminating Shimmervale. The kingdom was saved!

Mariposa and Catania looked at each other and gasped.

"Your wings!" exclaimed Mariposa.

"*Your* wings!" cried Catania. The fairies' wings had become larger, more colorful, and sparkly. Zee squealed with excitement as she and her friend wrapped each other in a huge hug.

Mariposa and Catania flew to the ballroom, where everyone had been freed from Gwyllion's spell.

"I'm so proud of you," King Regellius told Catania. Then he turned to Mariposa. "I owe you an apology. I misjudged you."

Gwyllion stirred in the corner. The king turned to punish the evil fairy, but Catania pulled him back. "You mustn't harm her," she said. "Remember why all this happened. Gwyllion asked us for one Crystallite. We have so many, but we said no."

Then Catania took off her own Crystallite necklace and asked Mariposa to put it around Gwyllion's neck. The Crystallite glowed with magic as Gwyllion was transformed into a good fairy.

"Thank you," said Gwyllion. Then, with a bow, she flew off.

A few days later, King Regellius and Princess Catania joined Mariposa in Flutterfield for a ball to celebrate the two lands coming together. Mariposa introduced them to Queen Marabella, Prince Carlos, and the other Butterfly Fairies. Then she and Catania and all their new friends danced the night away.